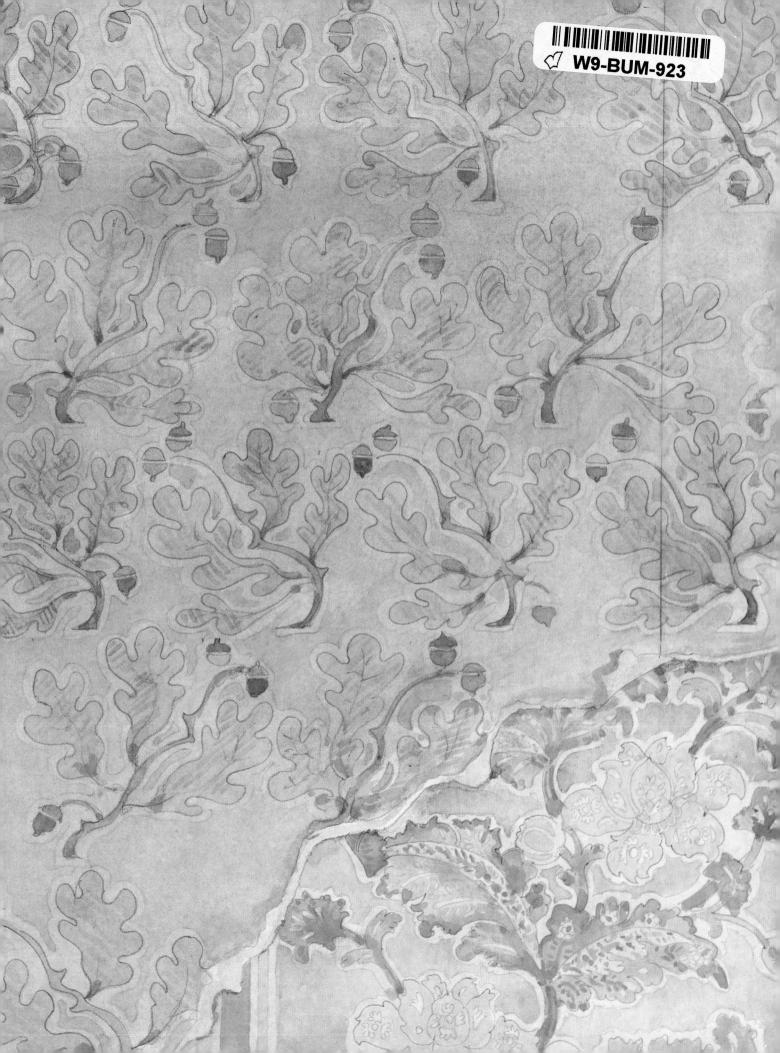

HOME PLACE

CRESCENT DRAGONWAGON

ILLUSTRATED BY

JERRY PINKNEY

MACMILLAN PUBLISHING COMPANY
NEW YORK

Text copyright © 1990 by Crescent Dragonwagon
Illustrations copyright © 1990 by Jerry Pinkney
Macmillan Publishing Company
866 Third Avenue, New York, NY 10022
Collier Macmillan Canada, Inc.
Printed in the United States of America   First Edition

10 9 8 7 6 5 4 3 2 1

The text of this book is set in 16 point Fournier.
The illustrations are rendered in pencil and watercolor on paper.
Library of Congress Cataloging-in-Publication Data
Dragonwagon, Crescent.
Home place/by Crescent Dragonwagon; illustrated by Jerry Pinkney.
– 1st American ed.   p.   cm.
Summary: While out hiking, a family
come upon the site of an old house and find
some clues about the people that once lived there.
ISBN 0-02-733190-3
[1. Dwellings — Fiction.] I. Pinkney, Jerry, ill. II. Title.
PZ7.D782Ho 1990 [E]-dc20 89-32911 CIP AC

For Ruth Eichor
–C.D.

To my father, James,
and in memory of my mother,
Willie Mae
–J.P.

Every year,
these daffodils come up.
There is no house near them.
There is nobody to water them.
Unless someone happens to come this way,
like us, this Sunday afternoon, just walking,
there is not even anyone to see them.
But still they come up, these daffodils
in a row, a yellow splash
brighter than sunlight, or lamplight, or butter,
in the green and shadow of the woods.
Still they come up, these daffodils,
cups lifted to trumpet
the good news
of spring,

though maybe no one hears
except the wind
and the raccoons who rustle at night
and the deer who nibble delicately
at the new green growth
and the squirrels who jump
from branch to branch
of the old black walnut tree.

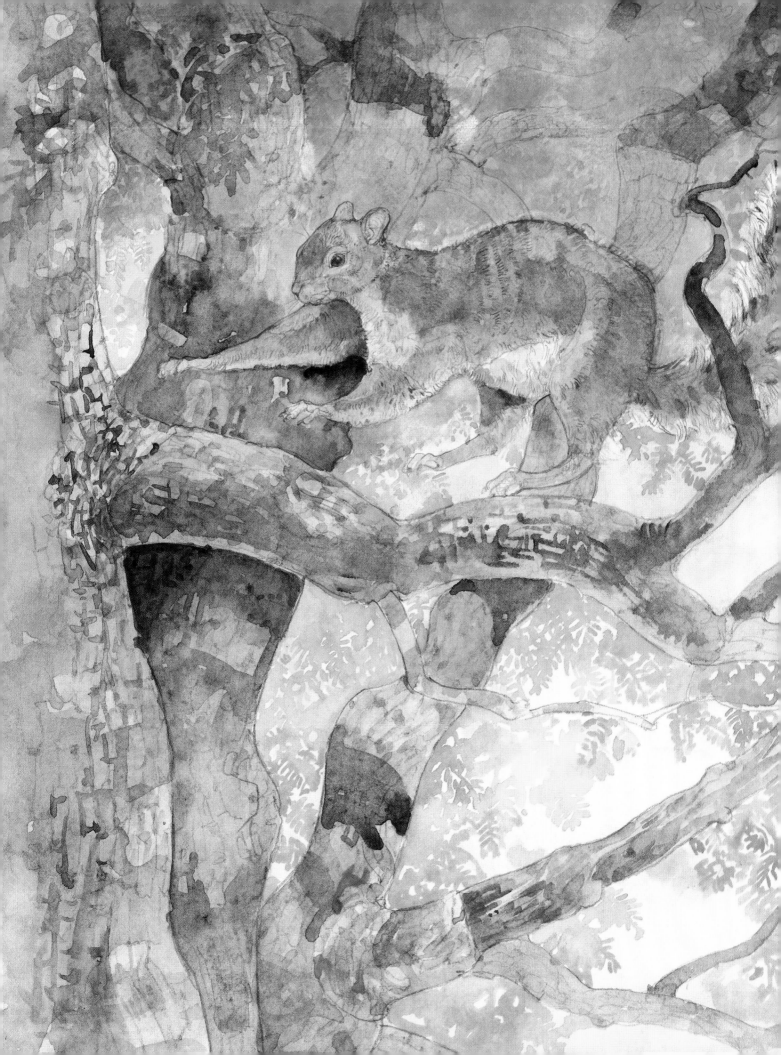

But once,
someone lived here.
How can you tell?
Look. A chimney, made of stone,
back there, half-standing yet, though honeysuckle's
grown around it—there must
have been a house here. Look.
Push aside these weeds—here's
a stone foundation, laid on earth.
The house once here was built on it.

And if there was a house, there was
a family.
Dig in the dirt, scratch deep, and what
do you find?
A round blue glass marble, a nail.
A horseshoe and a piece
of plate. A small yellow bottle. A china doll's arm.

Listen. Can you listen, back, far back?
No, not the wind, that's now. But listen,
back, and hear:
    a man's voice, scratchy-sweet, singing "Amazing Grace,"
    a rocking chair squeaking, creaking on a porch,
    the bubbling hot fat in a black skillet, the chicken frying,
    and "Tommy! Get in here this minute! If I have to call you
    one more time—!"
    and "Ah, me, it's hot," and "Reckon it'll storm?"
"I don't know, I sure hope, we sure could use it,"
    and "Supper! Supper tiiiime!"

If you look, you can almost see them:
the boy at dusk, scratching in the dirt with his stick, the
uneven swing hanging vacant
in the black walnut tree, listless in the heat;
the girl, upstairs, combing out her long, long hair, unpinning,
unbraiding, and combing, by an oval mirror;

downstairs, Papa washing dishes as Mama sweeps the floor
and Uncle Ferd, Mama's brother, coming in, whistling, back
from shutting up the chickens
for the night, wiping the sweat
from his forehead.
"Ah, Lord, it's hot, even late as it is,"
"Yes, it surely is."
Someone swats
at a mosquito.
Bedtime.

But in that far-back summer night,
the swing begins to sway
as the wind comes up
as the rain comes down
there's thunder there's lightning (that's just like now)
the dry dusty earth soaks up the water
the roots of the plants, like the daffodil bulbs
the mama planted, hidden under the earth, but alive
and growing, the roots
drink it up. A small green snake
coils happily in the wet woods,

and Timmy sleeps straight through the storm. Anne, the girl, who
wishes for a yellow hair ribbon, wakes, and then returns to
sleep, like Uncle Ferd, sighing as he dreams
of walking down a long road with change in his pocket. But
the mother wakes, and wakes the father, her husband,
and they sit on the side of the bed,
and watch the rain together,
without saying a word, in the house where everyone else
still sleeps. Her head on Papa's shoulder,
her long hair falling down her back, she's wearing
a white nightgown
that makes her look
almost like a ghost when the lightning flashes.

And now, she *is* a ghost, and we
can only see her
if we try. We're not sure
if we're making her up, or if
we really can see her, imagining
the home place as it might have been, or was, before
the house burned down, or everyone moved away
and the woods moved in.

Her son and daughter, grown and gone, her brother
who went to Chicago, her husband, even
her grandchildren, even her house,
all gone, almost as gone as if
they had never laughed and eaten chicken and rocked,
played and fought and made up,
combed hair and washed dishes and swept,
sang and scratched at mosquito bites.
Almost as gone, but
not quite. Not quite.
They were here.
This was their home.

For each year, in a quiet green place,
where there's only a honeysuckle-vined chimney
to tell you there was ever a house
(if, that is, you happen to travel that way,
and wonder, like we did);
where there's only a marble, a nail, a horseshoe, a piece
of plate, a piece of doll,
a single rotted almost-gone piece of rope swaying
on a black walnut tree limb,
to tell you there was ever a family here;

only deer and raccoons and squirrels
instead of people
to tell you there were living creatures;
each year, still,
whether anyone sees, or not,
whether anyone listens, or not,
the daffodils come up,
to trumpet their good news
forever and forever.

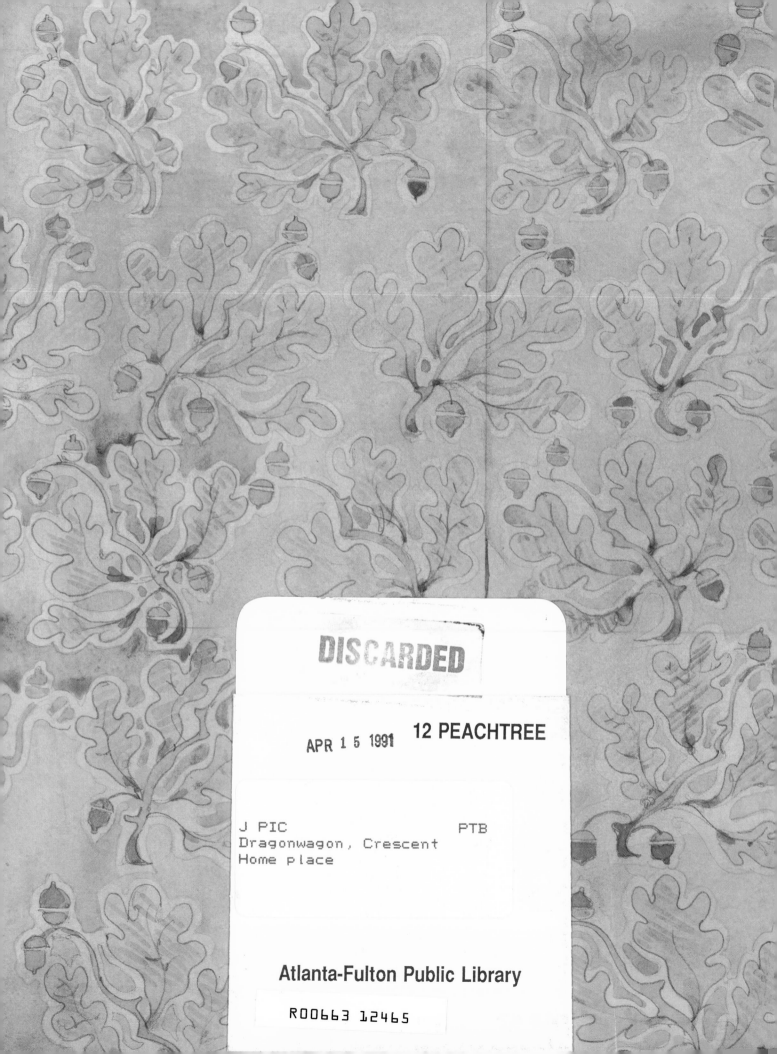